Blue Puts on a Play

Published by Advance Publishers, L.C.
www.advance-publishers.com

©2000 Viacom International Inc. All rights reserved. Nickelodeon,
Blue's Clues and all related titles, logos and characters are trademarks
of Viacom International Inc.
Visit Blue's Clues online at www.nickjr.com

Written by Ronald Kidd
Art layout by Niall Harding
Art composition by David Maxey
Produced by Bumpy Slide Books

ISBN: 1-57973-077-9

Blue's Clues Discovery Series

Hi! Come on in! Blue and I just finished reading "Goldilocks and the Three Bears."

Have you read it? You have? Great! 'Cause we're going to act it out and put on a play!

Blue wants me to play a special part. Cool! Which part do you want me to play, Blue?

Oh! Good idea! We'll play Blue's Clues to figure out which part you want me to play in "Goldilocks and the Three Bears." Will you help me? You will? Great!

While we're playing Blue's Clues, we can also get ready for our performance. Come on, let's go!

So we'll need three bears in the play. Hmmm, I wonder how we can make bear costumes. That's a great idea! Let's make bear masks!

Okay, what do we do first? Yeah! Color bear faces on pieces of cardboard, then cut them out. But how will the masks stay on? Good thinking! We'll use yarn to tie them on.

Well, how do they look? What's that? You see a clue? Oh, the yarn is a clue!

So we're trying to find out what part Blue wants me to play in "Goldilocks and the Three Bears," and our first clue is yarn. Hmmm . . . better find two more clues.

We'd better get our costumes and props together, too. Let's go look in the kitchen!

Cool! We're going to pretend soon, too! We're going to put on the play "Goldilocks and the Three Bears." Would you and Mr. Salt help us look for costumes and props?

Let's see . . . we'll need a dress for Goldilocks. Do you see anything we can use? Great idea! We can pretend the apron is Goldilocks's dress. This is great! We just started looking, and we already have a costume!

Yeah, you're right! Hmmm. Maybe we could find something that looks like a shawl. Do you see anything we could use? Oh, the tablecloth! Good job!

Thanks for your help, Mr. Salt and Mrs. Pepper. See you at the play!

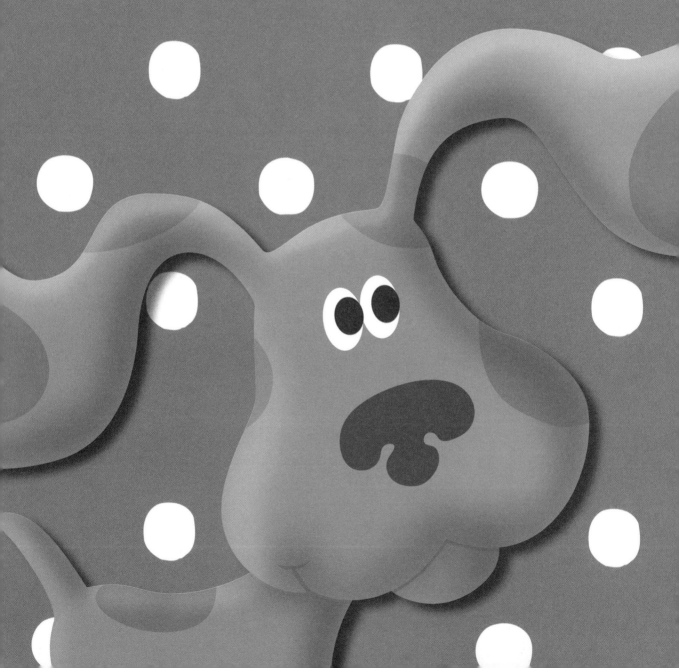

S-h-h-h! Tickety's sleeping. Let's be very
quiet while we're looking for props here. She
must have nodded off while she was reading
this book of fairy tales.

What? Oh, yeah! The girl on the book cover.
She must be our second clue.

Good pretending, Tickety! But we're glad you're awake, because we could use your help. We're putting on a play of "Goldilocks and the Three Bears," and we need some things we can use for the bears' beds. Can you think of anything in the bedroom we can use?

How about those pillows, Steve?

Yeah! The pillows can be the bears' beds!
Thanks, Tickety!

This is so exciting! We're going to put on a play, and our friends are here to help!
Will you be our audience? You will! Great!

What's that? You see a clue? Where? Oh, on the dress! That's our third clue! You know what that means, don't you? It's time to go to our . . . Thinking Chair!

Okay, we're trying to figure out what part Blue wants me to play in "Goldilocks and the Three Bears." Our three clues are yarn, a girl, and a dress.

That's it! Blue wants me to play the part of Goldilocks! We just figured out Blue's Clues! Cool!

Hey, we're ready to start the show! Well, thanks for helping us get ready for the play. And thanks for playing Blue's Clues!

BLUE'S EGG CARTON MASKS

You will need: scissors, egg cartons, colored markers, pipe cleaners, yarn, and a stapler

1. Ask a grown-up to cut individual cups out of the egg cartons to make animal noses.

2. Ask a grown-up to cut breathing holes in the bottom of each cup. Then staple a length of yarn to each side to hold the cup in place around your head.

3. Decorate the cups with colored markers to be the noses of cats, dogs, pigs, and other animals. Ask a grown-up to poke holes on either side of the cup. Stick pipe cleaner "whiskers" through the holes.

4. Try an animal on for size!